HAiBU

SAVES THE CIRCUS ANIMALS

Written by Blake Freeman
with Tara Price

Illustrated by Zoltan Boros and Gabor Szikszai

GRAPHIC ARTS
BOOKS®

LITTLE HAIBU chased after the dogs like she was in a battle. "I'll protect the village from these animals!" she roared. They tackled her and she laughed.

Haibu had a very special gift: she could speak with animals. She lived in a small village in the far north called Montooka, where they had a motto: Be Happy, Be Friendly, and Be Family.

One day Haibu went fishing and met a baby seal that was trying to eat all of her fish!

"Let's be friends," Haibu said to the seal. "I will call you Kanuux (kuh-new)."

All that fish attracted a giant polar bear.

"Oh no…" Haibu said as the polar bear got closer and closer, until…

Craaack! The bear's heavy weight broke the ice all around them.

Oh no! A chunk of ice broke off and Haibu and Kanuux floated out into the deep blue ocean.

"I can't swim back now," Haibu cried. "I'll freeze!" But Kanuux stayed by her side and kept her warm.

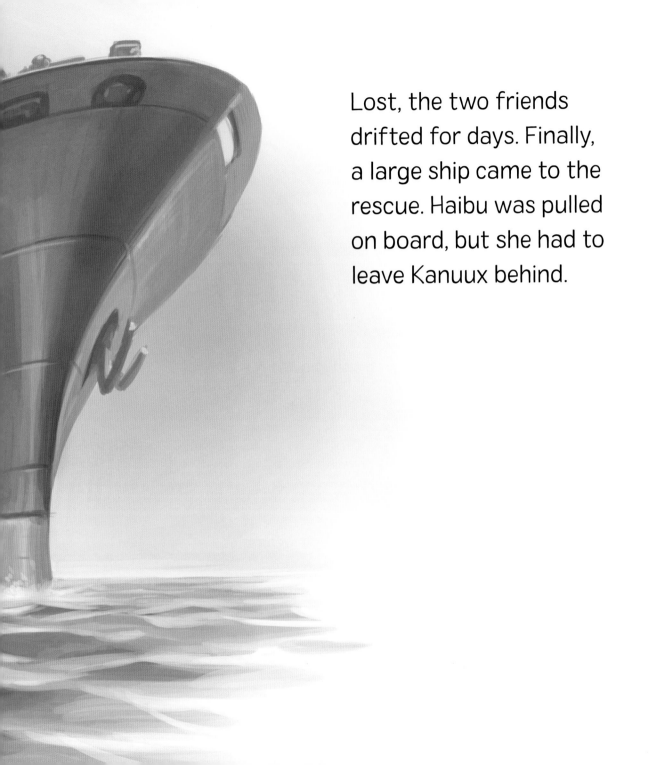

Lost, the two friends drifted for days. Finally, a large ship came to the rescue. Haibu was pulled on board, but she had to leave Kanuux behind.

When she woke up, Haibu was in an orphanage in New York City. She needed to find a way to get back to Montooka!

A boy tossed a peanut at her. "Hi, I'm Scotty!" he said.

Haibu looked at him. "My name is Haibu and I am lost. Can you please help me find my way home?"

The next morning at breakfast, Scotty introduced her to his other friends at the orphanage. "This is Haibu and she is lost. We have to help her get home!"

The gang put their heads together but couldn't come up with any ideas.

"I need a break," Haibu said. She and Scotty went outside.

They sat on a bridge and thought. Suddenly, Haibu cried, "Animals! Can you help me find some animals? They may know how I can get home."

"Sure," Scotty replied. "There's a circus near the Statue of Liberty. I can take you there!"

When they reached the circus, Haibu was upset to see the animals in cages. Scotty was amazed to see Haibu speak with the animals.

"Can you help me find my home?" Haibu asked.

"We can try," replied Eron the Lion.

"But you have to free us first," said Wiz the Elephant.

"We will do our best," replied Haibu.

They returned to the orphanage.

"We found a way to get Haibu back home," Scotty told their friends.

They came up with a plan to free the animals from their cages and reunite them with their families too.

"Every animal deserves to be free and happy!" Haibu shouted.

The day of the animal rescue arrived. The kids put their plan in motion.

Haibu and Scotty dressed like clowns to sneak into the circus, while the other kids dressed as truck drivers to bring everyone to safety. They were very nervous. If they got caught, the animals could be in those cages forever.

Haibu and Scotty sneaked into the tent. They watched the circus ringmaster whip the animals to get them to do tricks.

"Stop! You're hurting them!" Haibu yelled.

The circus workers looked at them. "Wait. Those aren't real clowns!" one said. "Get them!"

"Time to go!" Scotty yelled to Haibu.

Haibu and Scotty grabbed
the ringmaster's keys
and unlocked the cages.
Then they ran as fast
as they could!

They raced out to the
waiting trucks. The animals
were safe now—except
one. Wiz the Elephant
blocked the door to stop
the circus workers from
following them.

"Go without me!" Wiz yelled. "Save the others!"

Tears filled Haibu's eyes. "I will never forget you,
Wiz. I will be back for you very soon!"

Haibu and her friends were heroes! They were famous all over the world. Haibu's family found her and she could finally go home.

At the airport, the friends gave each other gifts and said goodbye. "Thank you for helping the animals," Haibu said.

"We won't forget you!" said her friends.

Back in Montooka, Haibu told Kanuux
about her adventure.

"We saved them all!" she said.
Kanuux gave her a high five.

Word spread quickly around
the world that animals had
finally found their voice.

And her name is Haibu.

This book is dedicated to everyone
who dared to dream and then took
a chance to turn that dream into a reality.

Library of Congress Control Number: 2019905565

ISBN 9781513262543 (hardbound)
ISBN 9781513262574 (e-book)

Printed in China
22 21 20 19 1 2 3 4 5

Published by Graphic Arts Books
an imprint of West Margin Press

WEST MARGIN PRESS

WestMarginPress.com

In Association with Admit 1 Studios
in partnership with WildAid

Download the Haibu app from your app store
to learn more, play more, and read more.

Find all things Haibu at www.haibu.love

Proudly distributed by Ingram Publisher Services

WEST MARGIN PRESS
Publishing Director: Jennifer Newens
Marketing Manager: Angela Zbornik
Editor: Olivia Ngai
Design & Production: Rachel Lopez Metzger